Puppy Tricks

by Dawn McMillan
illustrated by Sue O'Loughlin

Harcourt
SCHOOL PUBLISHERS

Requests for permission to make copies of any part of the work should be addressed to School Permissions and Copyrights, Harcourt, Inc., 6277 Sea Harbor Drive, Orlando, Florida 32887-6777. Fax: 407-345-2418.

HARCOURT and the Harcourt Logo are trademarks of Harcourt, Inc., registered in the United States of America and/or other jurisdictions.

Printed in China

ISBN 10: 0-15-351430-2
ISBN 13: 978-0-15-351430-2

Ordering Options
ISBN 10: 0-15-351212-1 (Grade 2 Advanced Collection)
ISBN 13: 978-0-15-351212-4 (Grade 2 Advanced Collection)
ISBN 10: 0-15-358065-8 (package of 5)
ISBN 13: 978-0-15-358065-9 (package of 5)

11 12 13 14 15   0940   15 14 13 12 11 10

"I wonder what it would be like to live in a home with a family," said Spot. "This pet store has been an excellent home so far, but we can't live here forever. I want a real home."

"I just know someone will buy us sooner or later," said Patch. "I just hope it's sooner!"

"Oh, dear! If we all get new homes, then we'll be separated!" moaned Boots.

"We might see each other when our families take us for walks," said Spot hopefully.

"Don't worry, Boots. You'll make friends in your new neighborhood," added Patch.

"I suppose so," sighed Boots glumly.

"Look, there's a family coming into the store," announced Spot, "and the little girl looks sad. We could cheer her up."

"Do you have any puppies for sale?" the girl inquired politely.

"Yes, we do," said the store assistant. "They're right over there, along the back wall."

"Eleanor's best friend moved overseas, so we thought a puppy might cheer her up," said Eleanor's mom to the assistant.

"We live in the country and have always wanted a dog," added Dad.

"They live in the country!" cried Spot.
"I must admit, I've always wanted to live in the country! What if we could convince Eleanor to take us all home? I have a plan."

Spot whispered his plan to the others as Eleanor's family walked toward them.

"Ow-ow-ow," howled the puppies all of
a sudden. Eleanor ran toward them.

"Mom, Dad," Eleanor laughed, "the puppies
are singing! Listen!"

"I'd barely call it singing!" chuckled Dad.
"It sounds more like yodeling!"

Next Patch rolled over and over, and Boots pranced along on her hind legs. Then the puppies used their noses to play ball with one another. They looked adorable.

8

"Now they're performing tricks," Eleanor giggled. "Aren't they hilarious?"

"Yes, they're definitely quite witty," agreed Mom. "They're also very cute."

Then the puppies huddled in the corner.
"This last part of the plan is extremely
important," said Spot quietly, in a serious voice.

The puppies began to stroll around the cage. Then, at exactly the same time, they all sat down and stared at Eleanor. They cocked their heads to one side and blinked their eyes.

"Oh, they're absolutely adorable,' said Eleanor. "I love the one with the black paws!"

Boots lowered her head onto her front paws, and Spot and Patch howled!

"They're all so cute," said Eleanor, "that I can't possibly choose just one of them."

Then Spot put his head on his paws, and Boots and Patch howled!

Mom grinned and said, "They're working as a team! Let's take them all!"

"What will we do with three puppies?" exclaimed Dad.

"We have plenty of space for dogs," Mom replied. "When they grow up, they can help on the farm."

"It's a great idea," cried Eleanor happily, "and I will help take care of them."

"Hurrah!" cried Patch.

"We're going to the country!" cheered Spot.

"Ow-ow-ow," sang Boots, "and we're going together!"

Think Critically

1. What did the dogs do to get Eleanor's family to take them home?

2. How did Eleanor change during the story?

3. What did Mom think the puppies could do when they grew up?

4. What types of jobs do you think the dogs could do on the farm when they are older?

5. If you could choose to have any animal from a pet shop, what would it be? Why?

 **Social Studies**

Write a Paragraph The story took place in a pet store. Write a paragraph to tell about why customers (buyers) might want to buy a pet and why the pet store owner (the seller) might be selling pets.

School-Home Connection Talk to family members about different types of pets. Talk about how each type of pet needs to be looked after.

Word Count: 496